So-Hee and Lowry

by Anna Kang   Illustrated by Christopher Weyant

two lions

So-Hee was lonely.

She didn't have a brother or a sister.

She didn't have many friends either.

What she did have was a mother who loved her

More than anything,
So-Hee longed for a pet
she could hold and love,
one who would love her back.

It seemed hopeless.

Until one day, So-Hee saw a sign. A giant sign.

You can borrow any of my books or toys anytime you want, OK? We share every—

AHHHH-CHOOO!!!

"Lowy?"

Lowy? Where are you?
It was just a sneeze . . .

I'm sorry if I scared you.
Please come back . . .

Lowy!

You are my best friend.

From that day on, So-Hee and Lowy were inseparable.

A scoop of ice cream and you'll be as good as new. Lowy, please bring in our next patient.

As spring warmed into summer . . .

summer cooled into fall . . .

and fall chilled into winter,
the one constant was So-Hee and Lowy.

But one icy morning,
Lowy was gone.

So-Hee was about to give up hope when . . .

HEELLPP!!

So-Hee didn't have a brother or a sister.

But she did have a lot of nice neighbors,

a mother who loved her,

and a few best friends.

May you find that special pet one day.
—A.K. & C.W.

Text copyright © 2025 by Anna Kang
Illustrations copyright © 2025 by Christopher Weyant

All rights reserved. No part of this book may be reproduced, or stored in a retrieval system, or transmitted in any form or by any means, electronic, mechanical, photocopying, recording, or otherwise, without express written permission of the publisher.

Published by Two Lions, New York
www.apub.com
Amazon, the Amazon logo, and Two Lions are trademarks of Amazon.com, Inc., or its affiliates.
ISBN-13 (hardcover): 9781542036658
ISBN-13 (ebook): 9781542036641

The illustrations are rendered in ink and watercolor with brush pens on Arches paper.
Book design by Abby Dening
Printed in China
First Edition
2 4 6 8 10 9 7 5 3 1